Reading BOROUGH COUNCIL

Reading (
Battle (
Caversha

CHRISTMAS CAROL
THE MOVIE

CHRISTMAS CAROL - THE MOVIE
A PICTURE CORGI BOOK : 0 552 54753 0

PRINTING HISTORY
Picture Corgi edition published 2001

1 3 5 7 9 10 8 6 4 2

Copyright © Illuminated Films (Christmas Carol) Ltd/The Film Consortium
Ltd/MBP - 2001
Text copyright © Narinder Dhami 2001

Designed by Ian Butterworth

Picture Corgi Books are published by Transworld Publishers,
61-63 Uxbridge Road, London W5 5SA,
a division of The Random House Group Ltd,
in Australia by Random House Australia (Pty) Ltd,
20 Alfred Street, Milsons Point, Sydney, NSW 2061,
in New Zealand by Random House New Zealand Ltd,
18 Poland Road, Glenfield, Auckland 10,
and in South Africa by Random House (Pty) Ltd,
Endulini, 5A Jubilee Road, Parktown 2193

Printed in Belgium by Proost

www.booksattransworld.co.uk/childrens

CHRISTMAS CAROL
THE MOVIE

Text by Narinder Dhami

PICTURE CORGI BOOKS

It was an icy Christmas Eve in Old London Town. Gabriel the mouse was running through the snow-covered street. He scurried inside the Alms Hospital for the Poor, where the sick children were cared for by Nurse Belle.

"Look!" shouted one boy. "Gabriel's back!"

Happy to see his old friends again, Gabriel performed a backflip, and the children laughed and clapped.

But there was one person who was never cheerful...

Ebenezer Scrooge.
"Merry Christmas indeed! Humbug!"

Scrooge was on his way to his office. But, for some reason he couldn't explain, he felt nervous. His heart pounded as he quickly looked around the dark, empty lane. Was there somebody there?

Scrooge hurried quickly to his office, where his clerk, Bob
Cratchit, was hard at work in his chilly little room. Ellen the office
mouse watched, as Scrooge entered his own, much warmer room.

Back at the hospital, Tiny Tim Cratchit was well enough to go home for Christmas.

"Keep him warm," Doctor Lambert told his mother. "He mustn't get that cough back."

Suddenly two men burst into the room. "Doctor Lambert?" one shouted. "We have come to take you to prison!"

Belle was horrified. And she was even more shocked to find that the hospital owed money to Mr Scrooge.

"*Ebenezer* Scrooge?" Belle gasped. She'd known him years ago...

Belle wrote a letter to Scrooge, begging for help. Then she
went with Gabriel to his office. When they discovered that
Scrooge was out, Gabriel hid under
Cratchit's desk to wait for his return.
He wanted to make sure that
Scrooge read the letter
straightaway.
Ellen looked
at the other
mouse curiously.

Scrooge was returning to the office, when he met his nephew, Fred.

"Will you come for Christmas dinner tomorrow, Uncle?" Fred asked cheerfully.

"Humbug!" Scrooge snapped, and shut the door in Fred's face.

He stomped upstairs, and slammed an account-book down on Cratchit's desk.

Gabriel was dismayed to see Belle's letter fall to the ground. He was climbing down the desk to retrieve it when –

SPLASH!

He fell headlong into a bucket of water.

Luckily, Ellen pulled Gabriel out just in time. For at that moment, Scrooge grabbed the bucket, and emptied it over some carol-singers standing underneath the window. Tiny Tim was one of them, and he was soaked to the skin.

Although it was Christmas Eve, Scrooge made Cratchit work late. It wasn't until Cratchit left that Scrooge spotted Belle's letter.

But what was that? It was a strange clanking sound...

Suddenly a ghostly figure appeared, draped in chains. It was Scrooge's dead business partner, Marley.

"I've come to warn you, Scrooge!" Marley moaned.

Scrooge was terrified.

"You'll be haunted by three ghosts!" Marley explained. "You must mend your ways…"

Scrooge was trembling as he hurried home. He didn't know that both mice were hiding in his coat pocket. But Scrooge fell asleep before he could read Belle's letter.

When he woke up again, a bright light filled the room, and there was the glowing figure of a girl.

"I am the Ghost of Christmas Past!" she announced. "Walk with me!"

Scrooge was forced to take the ghost's hand. Gabriel immediately jumped into the pocket of Scrooge's robe, but Ellen was left behind.

The ghost took Scrooge back in time to see his Christmas Past. First, they flew to his school, where Scrooge was sitting alone in a dormitory, crying because his father wouldn't let him go home for Christmas.

Then it was three years later, and Scrooge's sister arrived to take him home.

Scrooge and Fan hurried out to the carriage. Waiting for them was Fan's best friend... Belle.

The ghost then showed Scrooge more Christmases gone by. Scrooge and Belle danced together at a party, and promised that they would love each other always.

"What happened to those dreams?" the ghost asked, and Scrooge looked sad.

The scene changed again. Scrooge's father had died and left all his money to his son. Poor Fan died too, giving birth to Scrooge's nephew, Fred. But by now, Scrooge was a rich man. He had promised to marry Belle, but she came from a poor family. Scrooge said she must sign a marriage contract.

"I release you from our engagement!" Belle cried, running out of the room in tears. Scrooge could hardly bear to watch.

"I wish to see no more!" he cried. And suddenly, in a swirl of green fog, he was back in his own bedroom.

"It is over!" Scrooge said thankfully. "Humbug!"

Then he heard a cheerful, booming voice...

"I am the Ghost of Christmas Present."

It was the second ghost, a large man in a golden robe, carrying a glowing torch. "I have much to show you!"

This time both Gabriel and Ellen grabbed Scrooge's robe, and went with him. They flew over the snowy streets of London. Wherever the ghost shook his torch, he spread sparkles of Christmas cheer.

They stopped at Fred's house, where he and his wife and their
friends were having a very merry Christmas. Then they flew over
another street, where some men were taking
all the furniture from a woman's house.
The woman and her child were
crying bitterly.

"Merry Christmas from
Mr Scrooge!" said the men unkindly.

Scrooge felt full of shame as he
looked at the sad scene.

Then they flew on to see the Cratchit family having their Christmas dinner. Tiny Tim was coughing hard. His father wanted to drink to the health of Mr Scrooge, but Mrs Cratchit was furious.

"He threw a bucket of water over Tiny Tim!" she snapped. "He's a mean old man!"

Gabriel and Ellen were shocked.

"Will the poor boy live?" Scrooge asked the ghost anxiously.
"I know nothing of the future!" the ghost replied, and vanished.

Out of the mist, a third ghost appeared. He was tall and silent, with the body of a skeleton, the Ghost of Christmas Future. The two mice were terrified, and dived into Scrooge's pocket.

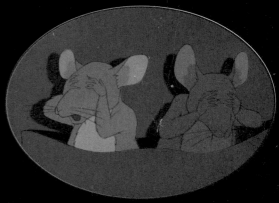

Scrooge watched closely as the Cratchit family appeared. They were sitting round the table again, but Tiny Tim wasn't there. They all looked very miserable.

"Oh!" Scrooge fell to his knees. There in front of him was a cold, lonely grave. *Here Lies Ebenezer Scrooge...*

"I can change!" Scrooge moaned. "Is it too late?"

B O N G !

The church bell rang out, and Scrooge opened his eyes. He was lying on his own bed, and he was alive!

"I'm alive!"
Scrooge danced a jig
round the room with
Ellen and Gabriel.
"And I *must* change..."

Ebenezer Scrooge *did* change.

He was reunited with Belle, and he used his money wisely to help the hospital. He was also reunited with his nephew, Fred, and often visited him and his wife. Scrooge even made Bob Cratchit his business partner.

And to Tiny Tim, who did *not* die,

he was a second father.

From that time on,

Scrooge kept Christmas

in his heart all through the year.

And what happened to
Ellen and Gabriel?
Well, they went on to have
many more adventures
together, because, after all,
who wants to spend their
life alone?